Buried Treasure in Nepal

Story by Melaina Faranda

Illustrations by Paulina Dybala

Contents

Chapter 1

Departure

Seth glanced up from flicking through the channels on the inbuilt screen in the headrest in front of him.

Rosie continued to tug at his arm. “Seth, all the buildings look like toy blocks!” she exclaimed, lifting the pirate eyepatch of her toy monkey, Bunky, so that he could see better, too.

Seth spoke in a monotone. “It’s because we’re so high up.” He returned to the screen and ignored his little sister.

"Seth, do you think you could try a little harder?" Mum asked. "It's her first time on a plane. And *our* first time being overseas together."

Seth shrugged, to remind her he was an unwilling participant. It was a matter of principle to him that Mum didn't think he was in any way okay about going away and being forced to drop the epic plans he'd made to go mountain biking with his friends over the holidays.

He reached again for the phone in his pocket and patted it with relief. Mum had felt guilty enough to let him bring it. While they were in Nepal visiting where Dad worked as a chief engineer on a hydroelectric power plant, the phone would be Seth's lifeline to his friends.

Seth was used to Dad working overseas. Whenever he came back, Dad would be grinning as he hefted suitcases stuffed with gifts out of the taxi. "Treasure for my greatest treasures," Dad would say. And for a little while after Dad got back, Seth would feel complete – him, Mum, Dad and Rosie all together again.

For the first days after Dad's return, the tight lines etched between Mum's eyebrows softened. Instead of Mum's usual pasta, there'd be laughter and new flavours in the kitchen as Dad showed Mum the new dishes he'd learnt how to cook while he was away. Mum would let Seth and Rosie stay up later, and she didn't mind as much if Seth forgot to empty the dishwasher.

Because there was always a bunch of saved-up stuff that needed fixing, Seth didn't feel he could take up any of Dad's time at home. Dad had got Seth into mountain biking before he'd started to work overseas, and Seth wished they could go and ride the bike trails together. He wanted Dad to be there for the competitions, especially when Seth won. But whenever he came home, Dad was always too busy.

Every time Dad flew out again, despite there being trails of new toys strewn by Rosie around every room, the house felt emptier. It was back to pasta most nights, and Mum trying to juggle her work

with driving Rosie to swimming lessons and Seth to the mountain bike trails.

So, a few weeks after Dad had flown back to Nepal last time, Seth had been surprised to see Mum smiling, as, barely glancing at the mess of Rosie's spilled breakfast cereal and milk, she made an announcement.

"Kids, I've got wonderful news – we're going to have a holiday with Dad, in Nepal!"

Seth shook his head. "No way. I'm not going." He already had plans for the school holidays. He wanted to enter the mountain biking championships and win another trophy. He couldn't care less about seeing some hydroelectric plant in Nepal.

At school, however, Ms Quinn had been way too excited about Seth's family adventure. "What an amazing opportunity. You're very lucky, Seth. I think this calls for a whole-class activity – we're all going to do a research project on Nepal!"

Thanks to his classmates, Seth now knew that Nepal was a tiny country squashed between the giants of India and China.

Seth discovered that Nepal was famous for having eight of the ten tallest mountains on Earth, including Mt Everest. Because it was landlocked, and the mountains were so high, it was hard for

Nepal to trade – there were no ships, few trains and hardly any decent roads, and it was one of the world's poorest countries.

Nepal was a very religious country, with a capital city called Kathmandu. Rhododendron flowers and cows were the national symbols. There were also tigers, snow leopards, elephants, rhinoceroses, yaks, monkeys and red pandas living in the wild.

Despite all that, Seth still didn't want to go to Nepal. He begged to be able to stay at his friend Abdo's place, but Mum ignored his pleading. Seth followed up with a no-talking tactic that was met with a seeming complete lack of awareness on Mum's part. Upping his protest to an eruption of rage, Seth slammed his bedroom door, only to have his favourite trophy fall off the shelf and snap in half.

Rosie didn't exactly help the cause. At dinner, between forking fried rice from her plate, she kept up a never-ending stream of chatter. "Are there pirates in Nepal?"

"No," Seth said flatly. "There's no sea for ships to sail on. It's a landlocked country."

Rosie seemed unfazed. "But they might still have buried treasure?"

"I doubt it."

"Can Bunky have his own seat on the plane?"

"No," Seth snapped. Then, seeing Rosie's expression crumple, he quickly explained, "Bunky might be scared and will need you to cuddle him."

As the days drew closer to their departure, Mum's voice became even more cheerful during her calls with Dad. She loved travelling to new places. It was how she and Dad had met – bungee jumping somewhere in Switzerland, before travelling together through northern Africa.

Seth, however, continued to refuse to go, while knowing he didn't have a choice. At least he was given one small win. Mum had finally agreed to let him have a phone while they were over there. It wasn't much, but it was something.

Chapter 2

Arrival

It was Seth's turn to sit by the window, and Rosie snuggled against his shoulder. Now that she was sleeping and not babbling about pirates and buried treasure, Seth felt that familiar squeeze of fondness in his chest that had first started when she'd been brought back from the hospital as a tiny baby.

A crescent moon, seemingly perfectly parallel with the plane, picked out hulking mountain silhouettes with a silvery sheen. Tiny lights glinted in the vast velvety blackness below as the plane began its descent into Kathmandu.

As Mum bundled them both down the plane stairs and across the tarmac, Rosie half-asleep, the first thing that struck Seth was the bracing coolness of the mountain air. Cold stung his cheeks, and he was relieved he'd put on his hoodie. A sharp tang of wood smoke drifted through the icy air, so different to the salty sea and lawn clipping aromas back home.

Dad was waiting for them, his arms wide open.

"Daddy!" Rosie shrieked, hurtling over to be swept up and turned in circles. Mum wasn't far behind. Dad eventually unpeeled them both and pulled Seth in for a bear hug.

Waiting patiently behind Dad was a young man in a neat little pink hat who pressed his palms together and raised them to his chest. "Namaste."

"This is Ram, our driver," Dad said. "Namaste means 'I bow to the spirit within you'. It's how Nepalese people greet each other."

Rosie pressed Bunky's paws together to mimic the gesture back to Ram.

The driver's eyes twinkled as he bent down to talk to Rosie. "I think your monkey will like visiting Monkey Temple to meet his friends. There are real monkeys there."

Rosie's eyes shone.

"We'll go there tomorrow," Dad promised. "We're going to spend the day in Kathmandu seeing the sights."

As Ram loaded their suitcases into the back of a jeep, Rosie asked if she could swap Bunky's pirate bandana for a hat like Ram's.

Ram's hat was called a topi, Dad said, and many men in Nepal wore them. "We'll look for a little one for Bunky when we go sightseeing."

As the jeep wound from the airport towards the city, dim lights shone from rectangular buildings webbed with a crazy tangle of overhead electrical wires. Every now and then came a dark gap between them, or tumbled ruins.

"What happened?" Seth asked.

Dad's tone was grim. "Earthquake. Some years back, but it was a bad one. Wiped out parts of Kathmandu. As if the people here didn't already have enough to deal with. That's why it's important I see this job out – people trying to rebuild after natural disasters need all the help they can get."

The hotel wasn't luxurious, but it also wasn't exactly making Seth think he was in one of the poorest countries in the world. After Ram helped lug all the suitcases up three flights of stairs, the first thing Seth asked for was an electrical plug converter and the Wi-Fi code – he wanted to charge his phone and see what was happening back home.

Mum shook her head in disbelief. "We've only just arrived!"

But Dad said, "Good idea. You'll probably want to take a bunch of photos with your phone tomorrow."

That night, it was comforting to hear the steady breathing of his family, the shifting of bedding as someone turned in their sleep, and Rosie's snuffling and occasional sighs beside Seth. He would never admit it out loud, but wherever they were, as long as they were all together, was where he belonged.

Chapter 3

Haggling

Seth felt sorry for the rickshaw driver. The wiry driver had a cloth tied around his forehead to soak up the sweat as he pedalled furiously to pull their carriage through the narrow lanes of Kathmandu. It could be hard enough riding your own bike, let alone towing a family of four! Seth wished his mountain biking friends could see this – none of them would ever complain about feeling the burn again.

Before getting onto the rickshaw, Dad had asked, "How much?" When the rider named a figure, Dad refused and named a lower figure, until finally they worked their way to an agreement.

Seth had felt embarrassed. Back home, you didn't argue about the price of things. You just paid what was asked.

"It's called haggling," Dad explained. "It's expected here. Prices can shift from moment to moment. Don't worry, I'll pay him more than a local would, but the first amount he asked for was too high."

"Did he want more than we can afford?" Rosie asked.

"No," Dad admitted. "But it was still more than I wanted to pay."

Rosie frowned. "But you said the people are poor, Daddy?"

Dad shifted uncomfortably. He quickly pointed to a statue covered in garlands of bright orange marigolds. "This is one of the shrines where people make offerings to their gods and goddesses."

Rosie was duly distracted, but Seth secretly smiled. His little sister had been spot on.

Kathmandu teemed with a snarl of honking vans and cabs that Dad called tuk-tuks. To cross the street, people had to risk a dangerous game of weaving through the chaos.

A woman with a bright orange shawl wrapped around her head and shoulders led a cow on a rope along the road. A bronze bell around the cow's neck occasionally chimed, while the traffic carefully swerved around them.

"Religion is very important here," Dad told them. "The Nepalese are mostly a mix of Hindus and Buddhists. For Hindus, cows are sacred. They would never consider hurting a cow, let alone eating one!"

Seth wondered what kind of animals the raw chunks of meat on the street stalls had come from. They weren't in neatly packaged containers, like back home in the supermarkets. Instead, each hunk of meat was exposed to the street's clouds of exhaust fumes, dust and buzzing flies. It was the same with people selling vegetables – carrots, cauliflowers, potatoes, tomatoes – all mounded and heaped on tables, or on mats set out on the ground.

Seth could tell that his father was relieved to get off the rickshaw. Dad handed over a wad of notes called rupees. When the driver reached into the money belt to fetch him change, Dad shook his head. “Keep it.”

They wandered into a large area in which some buildings were still damaged, or downright destroyed, by the earthquake.

“This is Durbar Square,” Dad said. “It has some of the oldest temples and palaces in Nepal.” He gestured to a dark red brick building. “In this temple there lives a young girl called the Kumari Devi, who has been specially selected as a living goddess.” He pointed up to one of the windows where a girl dressed in a bright red-and-gold costume and matching elaborate headdress gazed across the square.

Rosie’s eyes shone with longing. “She’s like a princess.”

Sensing a possible new obsession for his little sister, Seth said quickly, “I think being a pirate is way better. Princesses don’t get to find buried treasure. They have to worry about looking proper and keeping their clothes tidy all the time.”

But typically, Rosie had already moved on. She had spotted a passing Nepalese man in a topi. “Can we go and get Bunky a hat?”

The miniature pink topi they found in a nearby store suited Bunky. Rosie was doubly overjoyed when Ram drove them to Swayambhunath, a temple high on a hill. As they climbed the three hundred and sixty five steep steps, Rosie delighted in the mobs of monkeys that swung from brightly coloured cotton prayer flags, the babies piggybacking on their mothers or chasing each other to play tag.

"Monkeys are treated well here," Dad said. "In the Hindu religion, one of the gods – Hanuman – is the Monkey God."

Rosie looked thoughtfully at Bunky. He had gone from being a pirate with a patch to being Nepalese with a topi, and now …

"Don't go getting any big ideas," Seth warned.

Mum and Dad smiled at each other over Rosie's head, before bursting into laughter.

"Come on," Dad said, linking an arm through Mum's and reaching for Rosie's hand with the other. "I think we've had enough of the city, let's get out into the Himalayan mountains. I want you to see what I've been working on and why it's important. It's time you experienced the real Nepal."

Chapter 4

The Gods of Good Luck

It didn't look so far on the map, but Dad explained that what would be a simple three-hour car trip back home could take over ten hours in Nepal.

As they drove through the broad sweep of Kathmandu Valley, ringed by towering blue mountains, they passed whitewashed mudbrick farmhouses. Rows of ripening pumpkins lined the roofs and sheaves of corn hung from the eaves. People sat in doorways, sifting rice or combing their hair, while children played outside. Women in brightly coloured saris carried bundles of firewood on their backs, and men walked alongside ploughs yoked to huge bulls that Dad said were called bison.

As the jeep started to climb, Seth soon realised why the trip was going to take so long. Foothills ascended to giant jagged stone mountain walls. The road clung to the mountainsides in a perilous series of hairpin turns around cliffs, with scree tumbling to the silvery ribbons of rushing rivers in the ravines below. It was way scarier than any mountain bike trail Seth had ever ridden.

Rattling along, the jeep periodically hit potholes. Occasionally, Ram slammed on the brakes, sending everyone pitching forward only to be snapped back by their seat belts. In each instance, Seth saw that a small white painted stone had been used to mark that a section of road had broken away, leaving only a single narrow lane hugging the mountainside.

At times, it seemed they might collide with buses barrelling around the blind corners of the endless mountain bends. The buses blared tinny music and were bedecked with flower garlands and tinselly charms hanging from every part of the windscreen. The front of their own jeep was similar. The charms were for good luck, Ram had explained, patting the jeep's dashboard with its array of gods and goddesses.

Seth hoped the good luck would hold. Several times, through all the twists and turns, there were moments when the jeep and buses were barely scraping past each other.

The trip was even worse for Mum. In the middle seat, sandwiched between Seth and Rosie, Mum turned increasingly green-faced. "Stop, we have to stop," she finally called out. "I need some air!"

At a roadside stall, Ram bought snacks and offered them around. Seth took a packet of what looked like corn chips, tore it open and put one in his mouth.

His whole mouth and tongue felt like it was on fire. "It's …" he choked.

Dad read the packet. "This word means 'hot'," he said, pointing it out. He tousled Seth's hair. "Next time, stick with the peanuts."

Ram had dashed back to the stall and bought a mug of something warm and milky that smelled like cinnamon. "Chai," he said. "Drink."

While Seth drank the warm sweet tea and tried to breathe normally again, he heard Ram worriedly conferring with Dad. Together, they gazed up at the brilliantly blue sky. There wasn't a speck of cloud in sight. "They say there will be big rain," Ram said.

Dad shrugged. "We'll be all right. If we keep going, we should be there before nightfall."

Ram shook his head, his brow creasing with concern. "I think it's not good to keep going up the mountain. The road …" He didn't need to say any more. They had all seen the landslips and where part of the roads had simply washed away.

Dad looked put out. This clearly hadn't been in his plan.

"Only a small way along is my cousin's village," Ram offered. "There is enough room, and we can stay there. Then, in the morning, we go up the mountain."

Seth thought about the small white rocks marking each landslip, and the gods of good luck jamming the jeep's dashboard. "Dad, if Ram doesn't think it's a good idea, we should listen to him."

Chapter 5

A Warm Welcome

Ram's cousin's village turned out to be two single lines of houses divided by the road. One row of houses sat squarely against the mountain, rising steeply above, while the other perched above a series of terraced gardens that stretched to the river below.

Madhav and Ranju, Ram's cousin and his wife, lived in a house backing the mountain. The doors and window frames of their two-storey home were painted bright blue, and the whitewashed house appeared as if it had been built from rocks and stones from the river bed that snaked beneath the slope where the village perched.

Outside on the porch, an old lady beamed a toothless smile from where she sat in the sunshine, sorting a pile of scarlet chillies on a square of woven cloth.

Lying close by, a big shaggy dog slumbered, snoring away. Ram shook his head in disgust. "Lazy! It's the dog's job to protect the goats from the tigers."

"Really?" Seth asked.

Ram nodded. “Last year, Madhav said a tiger came right into the village. The women were afraid to let the children out, or even go to the river to do their washing.”

It didn’t look as if they were so afraid now. As the family walked further into the village, Seth saw kids of all ages outside playing a game using stones, with lines drawn by sticks in the dirt.

A small girl shyly reached out to touch Bunky, before showing Rosie the tiny baby goat she was leading with a twisted rope. Before long, the two girls were playing some complicated make-believe game out by the porch. Knowing Rosie, it no doubt involved pirates and buried treasure, and now, monkey gods. They both happily chattered in their own languages as they played, while chickens strutted alongside.

Madhav and Ranju warmly welcomed everyone into their home. Their eyes were wreathed with laughter lines, and broad smiles lit up their tanned faces.

Ranju’s baby was bound to her in a sling made from a long piece of cloth, but it didn’t seem to affect the slow grace with which she fetched mugs and poured them all boiling water from a big iron teapot on a clay-covered stove.

A warm citrus fragrance greeted Seth's nostrils – lemon tea. Ranju opened a packet of biscuits and offered them about, while Ram and Madhav spoke together worriedly in Nepali.

As if suddenly remembering they were there, Ram broke off to address Seth's parents. "My cousin says they think there will be a cloudburst. There will be too much rain in the one place. They worry because many things like this happen now. It is not like it was."

"Is it because of climate change?" Seth asked.

"There's a lot more melted snow and ice than there used to be," Dad said. "And the monsoon season has become worse – the rain is torrential." He gestured beyond the door to the opposite mountain rising steeply across the river. "As you can imagine, the landslides here are disastrous."

Ram added, "The people in the village worry because of the dam further up the river. If it fills too quickly, then the wall might break."

"You have to hope the engineers did their job properly," Dad said. He turned back to Seth. "Nepal is not only one of the poorest countries in the world, but its geography also creates weather that makes farming quite challenging. Just when the Nepalese are ready to harvest, a cloudburst or snap freeze might wipe out their crops. Not only that, now they're also dealing with earlier snow melt and thaw. In some areas, if people don't get their kids out of the villages in time to board in town before the rivers become uncrossable, the kids don't get to go to school."

Secretly, Seth thought not being able to go to school wouldn't be such a terrible thing.

"It is a hard life being a farmer and not having enough to eat," Ram chipped in. "It is education that gets us good jobs." He gestured to Dad. "That is why we are happy you are here. When we have electricity, we have more opportunities."

Ram winked at Seth. He could hardly have failed to notice how Seth constantly checked his phone for reception. "Then everyone can have a phone and go on the internet. We learn more and can get better jobs."

Rain suddenly pounded the roof. There were shouts outside, and the door was flung open. A soaked Rosie dashed back in, followed by the old lady with her hastily-bundled cloth full of chillies.

Ranju prepared their dinner, politely refusing help when they offered.

They all sat together on mats on the floor in the glow from the kerosene lamps and the clay-covered fireplace that Ranju periodically fed with dried cowpats.

Ranju seemed to take extra care with the old lady, plumping a cushion on the floor for her and serving her as if she might be a queen.

Seeing Seth's curiosity, Dad said quietly, "The Nepalese don't have retirement homes or nursing homes. The old people are treated with great respect. They have the most authority."

Everyone was given a metal tray with sections moulded into it. In one was a heaped mound of rice. In another, a scoop of yellow lentils. In a third was some kind of green spinach vegetable. Then, in a smaller indent, there was a spoonful of some type of pickle or chutney.

"This is called dahl baht," Dad said. "It's the national dish – dahl and rice."

There were no knives, forks or spoons. "Only use your right hand to eat," Dad whispered. "The Nepalese consider it unclean to eat with your left hand. Also, if you eat everything on the tray, it's like saying you want more. They're very generous, and they will keep heaping more food on it, even if it leaves them short. Remember to leave a little bit leftover, to say you've had enough."

After dinner, a colourful lumpy cotton quilt was laid out near the fire as a mattress for Seth and Rosie. Ranju worked on a belt she was weaving from colourful threads, while Mum, Dad, Ram and Madhav spoke together in English.

Madhav and Ranju had insisted on giving their own bed to Mum and Dad, who tried to refuse, without success. The couple said they would sleep on the floor in the room next door that belonged to Madhav's elderly mother. Ram would stay at a neighbour's house a few doors along. "It is Nepalese custom," Ram said proudly, "to give our guests the best of what we have."

Rosie fell asleep almost instantly, peacefully cuddling Bunky. But Seth struggled to sleep. They were snug and warm inside, and he could hear the murmur of his parents in conversation with Ram and Madhav. But the noise of the rain hammering the slate roof, meeting with the angry roar of the rising river below, was unsettling, and nothing like he'd ever experienced before. Seth wondered what his mountain biking friends would think about some of these roads. Would they be game to ride them? He rummaged in his pocket for the comforting smoothness of his phone – as if it could transport him back home again. So much for keeping him connected. There had been no reception for most of the day while they had been driving, and he was unsurprised to find that there wasn't any reception in the village, either.

Chapter 6

Landslide

Seth woke to a terrible sound. A rumble that became louder and louder. From the faint light of the dying embers in the clay fireplace, he could see Rosie's small sleeping form curled beside him. He scooped her closer as the sound became increasingly deafening.

Then, the landslide hit.

It felt as if the world had turned upside down. A dank stench of dirt suddenly filled the house, and the light from the fire was entirely blocked. When Seth reached out, he could feel an icy slick of mud. It had swallowed everything they had left beside the mattress – including their shoes.

In pitch darkness, Seth fumbled for the phone in his pocket and turned it on. He swiped for the flashlight function. A tide of mud and rocks had swept through the house. From somewhere outside, he heard a woman screaming. Then, other screams and shouts.

Seth realised that the wooden steps leading upstairs to where his parents had been sleeping were entirely engulfed by mud. "Mum, Dad!" he yelled. "Mum, Dad!"

There was no reply. He thought he might have heard a baby wailing. Was it Ranju's baby? But everything was blocked by the mud that had poured through the house. When he pointed his phone towards the front door, there was only a tiny sliver of black night beyond the mountain of mud.

His shouting had woken Rosie. "Seth?"

"I'm here." Seth pulled her against him.

Rosie patted about and held up a tiny pink hat. "Where's Bunky?" She started to sob.

"Shush, shush." He soothed her. "It's okay, Rosie, I'm going to get us out of here." He cast the light about desperately, pointing it towards where the stairs had been. Were their parents up there? Had they been swept up in this swamping river of mud and stones? He couldn't let himself think about it. What they would want most would be for him to make sure Rosie was safe.

Another terrifying rumble and screams from outside drove him into action. He thrust his phone at Rosie. "Hold this and point it there. I'm going to get us out."

Launching himself onto the small hill of rocks and dirt that blocked the door, Seth picked up a sharp-edged rock and frantically scraped at the mud nearest the top. When he had cleared a narrow squeeze hole, just large enough for him and Rosie to wriggle out of, he dashed back to her. "Hurry!"

"But, Bunky," Rosie wailed. "I can't leave him."

"We'll come back for him later," Seth lied. He half-dragged her up along the mud pile. "I'm going to get out and then pull you through, okay?"

Rosie nodded tearfully.

Seth threw himself onto the top of the pile and used his hands to try to scrabble and pull himself along the mud, through the doorway. It was so narrow that an adult would never have fitted through.

Once outside, he reached his hands back and yanked Rosie through, ignoring her protests as she was bumped along the top of the mud.

The rain had temporarily stopped. But the lack of stars, or the crescent moon he'd admired from the plane just a couple of days ago, must mean there were still rain clouds in the sky. Above the sound of the rushing river, Seth could hear crying and people shouting out. A few lanterns wove through patches of darkness, picking out scenes of mud-strewn chaos. A whole chunk of the looming mountain above, a great earth river of dirt and stones, had become sodden and simply slid away from the core of rock beneath.

The top windows of Madhav and Ranju's house were shrouded in darkness. One set of windows swung open brokenly and mud oozed out. Seth wanted to go back and find his parents, but the way was blocked.

As if sensing Seth's panic, Rosie shrieked, "I want Mummy and Daddy!"

Seth forced himself to keep his voice steady. "Mum and Dad are okay, Rosie. They want me to look after you."

A woman with a lantern beckoned to Seth. "You speak English?" she asked.

Seth nodded.

"You must come with us. Not safe."

"But my parents are in there!" Seth pointed back to Madhav and Ranju's mud-choked house.

The woman frowned. She gestured to Rosie, whose tears had cut pale trails down her grubby cheeks. "It is too dangerous in the night, and there will be more rain. We will come back tomorrow."

She was right. As much as he wanted to stay and find their parents, he knew he needed to get Rosie to a safe place. Seth nodded reluctantly. "Come on, we need to go somewhere we can get you warm and dry."

Chapter 7

A Long, Painful Walk

Holding tightly to Rosie's hand, Seth joined the woman in a procession of people shuffling along in silent shock. Some carried bulging bundles wrapped in cloth. Others were empty-handed. Some people led goats or donkeys, and a few even led hulking bison. Seth and Rosie were both barefoot, and the icy mud and sharp stones beneath their feet were slippery and painful.

Together, everyone trudged along a narrow winding path.

"Where are we going?" Seth asked.

"To the next village," the woman explained. "It is on the top of the mountain, so there is no danger there."

The rain started again, at first lightly spitting, but then becoming a downpour. People slipped and slid along the steep muddy path, some dropping to all fours to crawl across sections where there had been smaller landslides.

Rosie tried to keep up beside Seth and eventually stopped asking for Mum or Dad, or complaining about how much her feet hurt.

At a pyramid-like tumble of rocks with rain-soaked prayer flags hanging limply from string, a man overtook them. He had a woven cane basket on his back, with the strap tied around his forehead. Inside the basket, legs dangling from the woven holes, were two children.

After Rosie stumbled and fell for the third time, Seth took a deep breath. "I'll give you a piggyback," he offered.

It was a steep mountain path that zigzagged upwards, and Rosie was heavier than she looked. When a man with a donkey saw Seth struggling, he indicated that Seth could put Rosie onto the donkey's back.

Grateful beyond belief, Seth tripped alongside Rosie and the donkey, focusing on the comforting warmth and musky smell of the donkey's fur and trying desperately not to think about what had just happened, and what might be coming next. The most important thing was to get Rosie to safety.

It felt like many hours of climbing before Seth spotted a few glowing windows ahead. The rain had stopped. There were shouts and confused commotion as sleepy villagers poured out to welcome the exhausted mud-stained refugees.

Even though Seth and Rosie were streaked with dirt and grit, the villagers quickly realised they were not Nepalese. The two of them were ushered towards a house and set in front of a fire, where they were wrapped in soft yak wool shawls. Seth gulped when he saw that, for the entire journey up the mountain, Rosie had been holding Bunky's little topi.

The women of the house boiled water and tenderly wiped the mud from their hands, feet and faces. Seth's feet were covered in grazes, as too, he saw, were Rosie's. The women dabbed at their grazes with some fluid that burned, before giving them each felt slippers that must have belonged to their own children. A mug of sweet tea was pressed into Seth's frozen hands.

"I need to find my parents!" Seth repeated with increasing volume, looking from one confused and concerned face to another. "I have to go back down and find them!"

Finally, the woman who had spoken English to Seth back in the village below was brought to the house.

"It is too dangerous," she told Seth. "We are on top of the mountain, where it is safe. When it is morning, we will go back and look for them. You will come, too."

Just before dawn, Seth slithered from Rosie's sleeping grip and crept to the window. They were on a broad plateau. Surrounding them were the taller, snow-capped peaks of the Himalayas, now lit a brilliant pink-gold. Apart from a rooster crowing, the morning was still, and the sky was clear, revealing the last sprinkling of stars. It was deceptively peaceful.

Seth slid open the door bolt and tiptoed across the icy road, closer to the edge of the plateau. Far below, the river was a ribbon of muddy froth. The mountainside was now scarred with ugly pale streaks, where sections had collapsed and tumbled towards the river.

Somewhere, beneath one of those giant streaks, might be his parents.

Chapter 8

The Rescue Party

Seth was to return to the devastated village with a rescue party of men and boys. He was assured, through a series of gestures, that Rosie would be looked after here at the house by the women.

Someone gave him an ill-fitting pair of old sneakers and a spade, and he joined the procession back down the mountain. Men and boys were laden with spades, hoes, rope and buckets, and anything that could be used for digging through thousands of tonnes of mud.

Other boys around Seth's age seemed full of the energy of a big adventure. But, as Seth shouldered his spade, he couldn't begin to feel anything but terror that nothing and no one could survive being buried by a mountain.

Now that it was daylight, he saw how close any of them might have been to dying last night on the perilous winding path. At certain points, the path was just centimetres from cliffs and sheer drops. A simple stumble could have sent someone plummeting over the edge and down into the river, hundreds of metres below.

Seth used the spade to steady himself. There were small landslips everywhere that were slippery and treacherous, and required careful manoeuvring. A single wrong-footed moment could potentially cause a tumble of scree and start an avalanche.

When they finally arrived at the village, it was barely recognisable. Some houses were still fully intact, with chickens scratching about and dogs lapping from puddles. Others had mud still slowly oozing through their doors and windows.

People were already clambering about, digging out doorways. Occasionally, a muffled shout for help could be heard, and people rushed towards it.

Seth marched straight to Madhav and Ranju's house. It was even worse than he had thought – nearly every opening was clogged with dirt.

He stood outside, shouting for his parents, until some of the men took pity on him. One of them took a spade and began to shovel out mud from the narrow hole Seth had made at the top of the doorway the night before.

The man finally broke through but returned within minutes, grim-faced and not meeting Seth's eyes.

"You have to find them!" Seth sobbed. "Please, please – try again! They're in there." He pointed to the window above.

Someone came racing over. It was Ram! He was okay! He spoke rapid Nepalese to another man, who dashed off and swiftly returned with a ladder made from bamboo poles lashed together.

Ram propped the ladder against the house and climbed up, dislodging the mud spilling from the upper-floor window with a shovel. Then, with a shout of excitement, he started tearing at the earth with his bare hands.

It took a team of men each taking turns, but, after what seemed like hours, there was a cheer. Shortly after, Mum appeared at the window, tear-stained and smeared with mud and scratches. Then, moments later, Dad.

Mum clung to Seth as if she'd never let go. "Where's Rosie?"

"Rosie's safe," Seth said, gasping for breath. "She's in the village up the mountain."

He finally managed to disentangle himself, only to be grabbed by Dad and pulled into another squeezing hug.

Dad explained that he had woken to the sound of the thunderous rumbling and had yelled for Mum to get under the bed. They had lain beneath as mud snapped the slate roof tiles and poured in through a widening gap in the eaves. When it finally settled, the bed had formed an air pocket and chamber around them. Neither had dared speak aloud their fears for Rosie and Seth, but both had immediately started digging with their hands, all night long, hoping they were digging in the direction of the window. They had only just poked a hole through, when they heard scraping and digging coming from the outside, and then Seth, shouting for them to be found.

With the other men, Dad helped dig a tunnel into the next room. Although in shock, Madhav, Ranju, the baby and Madhav's mother were all alive.

Seth and his parents spent the rest of the day joining in with the rescue effort, before the final challenge of having to walk back up the mountain. Yet something strange and new energised them – a sense of purpose and the elation of having survived. The climb was difficult, but not as hard as it had been last night.

"I can't believe I tried to carry Rosie," Seth said, as they panted their way up.

"Son," Dad said, for what must have been the hundredth time that day, "I am so proud of you. She's lucky to have such a brother."

Seth looked away, embarrassed to see such raw shining pride in his father's eyes. "I just wish we could have found Bunky," he said.

When they reached the village at the top of the mountain, people poured out, anxious to hear news of friends and family members from the village below. The family were welcomed back into the home Seth and Rosie had slept in the previous night.

While Rosie tearfully flung herself at their parents, Seth sat by the fire in front of an enormous tray of dahl baht. He greedily scooped it all up, then ate a second helping and a third. From across the crowded room, Dad nodded hearty approval.

Chapter 9

Home

After everything that had happened in the first two days, the rest of their trip was hardly a holiday, but Seth had stopped caring about missing out on mountain biking with his mates. Wherever Mum and Dad and Rosie were – that was home. They were all crammed in one room, helping with the recovery effort. Dad organised with his workplace to bring in a crew and heavy-duty machinery to help clear up and rebuild, while Mum campaigned for donations from home – leaving Seth to fill in for Bunky in Rosie's games.

He had gone back to the house several times, in the forlorn hope of finding that silly toy monkey, but Madhav and Ranju's house was one of many still to be fully cleared.

As the time drew nearer for them to depart, Seth became quieter. They had all come so close to losing each other, and he didn't want to say yet another goodbye to Dad.

It was Dad who approached Seth, while he stood watching an excavator push away piles of rubble in the village. Ever since the disaster, Dad had sought Seth out – including him in discussions about the rescue effort, and even asking for his opinions.

But still, Seth was surprised to hear Dad say, "How do you feel about me staying here for longer when you all go home?"

Dad had never asked him anything like this before. Two weeks ago, all Seth would have wanted to reply was, "I want you to come home. You always act like other people and other things are more important than being with us, with me, and I miss you." But now, Seth realised just how stretched Dad was between his family and work. This wasn't just a job for Dad – he cared deeply about making a difference.

Taking a deep breath, Seth gestured around. "We need you, Dad, but Madhav and Ranju and the village need you more."

Dad's voice sounded choked as he put his hand on Seth's shoulder. "Thank you for understanding. Five more months, then I promise I'll find work at home."

***

This time, there was no waiting for the slamming door of a taxi. Mum had driven Seth and Rosie to the airport to greet Dad. The village in Nepal had been rebuilt. Dad's role at the hydroelectric plant was almost ready to wrap up, and he had been able to hand it over to someone else.

He was finally coming home.

As Dad appeared through the sliding doors, he didn't have the usual bulging suitcases full of gifts. Instead, he was holding up something small – its little face a matted brown circle, with round ears and mud-scratched eyes.

Rosie squealed. "Bunky!"

Seth grinned at his little sister, then at his parents. "It looks like there was buried treasure in Nepal after all."